Brody was a Cowboy

Brody was a Cowboy

JEAN EDGAR

Illustrated by Jim Webb

Xulon Press
2301 Lucien Way #415
Maitland, FL 32751
407.339.4217
www.xulonpress.com

© 2022 by Jean Edgar

Illustrations by Jim Webb

Paperback ISBN-13: 978-1-6628-4512-3
Hard Cover ISBN-13: 978-1-6628-4979-4
Ebook ISBN-13: 978-1-6628-4513-0

"Children are God's love-gift; they are heaven's generous reward." Psalm 127:3

There are many ways to express love to our children. My hope is that Brody provides yet another opportunity for the reader to do just that! When I wrote *Brody Was a Cowboy*, I had every little boy's momma in mind mainly because of my first grandson, Hunley, who was "all boy" and loved by all. When I published the story eight years later, I had my youngest grandson, Titus, in mind. Titus embodies every emotion I felt creating Brody's story! (I even sent his photo to my wonderful illustrator for inspiration!) So, for David Hunley Kinard, Titus Marshall Edgar, and all mommas who love their little boys (and girls!), I hope this story makes you smile!

Brody was a cowboy!

He rode a spotted Bay,
and lassoed everything in sight.
Oh how he loved to play!

**Two shiny pistols on his hips,
he wore from dusk till dawn...**

Until his mom removed them,
when he began to yawn.

A big white hat he wore so proud,
high upon his head.

His boots, they were a bit too big.
"But they help me ride!" he said.

Cowboys are rough and tough,
They rope and ride all day!

Brody was a cowboy!

Brody was a fireman!

His truck was red and fast!

The siren was his favorite thing,

He loved to hear it blast!

**His raincoat kept him really dry,
while he'd put out a fire.**

**With his faithful garden hose,
he'd run till he would tire.**

There was no job too big for him.

Brody was so brave!

He worked so hard for hours on end.

There were always lives to save!

Brody was a fireman.
He was the very best!
"Chief" was the name you'd see
him wear proudly
on his chest.

BRODY WAS A SOLDIER!
He stood so straight and tall!
He was so cute,
looked like his dad,
uniform and all!

Through the jungle he would go.
Brody had no fear!

His backpack full of Debbie cakes.
All part of his soldier's gear.

"Sir, yes Sir!" you'd hear him shout
in his loudest voice.

For our great country he
would fight.

It was this soldier's choice!

Brody was a soldier,
It was clear to see.
A little man with a great big heart,
The best that he could be.

Brody was a five year old,
A boy who loved to play.

He was the greatest cowboy!
Yippy-yi-O-ki-Yay!

He was the best brave fireman
that you have ever seen!

And Brody was a soldier.
He was tough but never mean.

But best of all,
at least to Mom,
Brody was her boy.

And everything that Brody was
filled her heart with joy.

XXOO

CPSIA information can be obtained
at www.ICGtesting.com
Printed in the USA
LVHW070739150622
721318LV00005B/164

9 781662 849794